WALLACE, K.

Dr. Barnardo's boys

First published in 1999 by Franklin Watts
96 Leonard Street, London EC2A 4XD

Franklin Watts Australia
56 O'Riordan Street, Alexandria, Sydney, NSW 2015

This edition published 2002

Editor: Claire Berridge
Designer: Jason Anscomb
Consultant: Dr Anne Millard, BA Hons, Dip Ed, PhD

A CIP catalogue record for this book
is available from the British Library.

ISBN 0 7496 4597 0 (pbk)

Dewey Classification 362.7/941.081

Printed in Great Britain

Dr. Barnardo's Boys

by
Karen Wallace

Illustrations by Martin Remphry

W
FRANKLIN WATTS
NEW YORK • LONDON • SYDNEY

1

A Leap of Faith

Toby Cutler lay flat on the deck of a rotting Thames cargo boat. The man he knew as Black Bob looked up from the tiller and glared into the wet night.

"I knowsh you're about, young varmint," snarled Black Bob. His voice was harsh and slurred from the rum he had been drinking all evening. "And when I find ye, I'll give 'ee summat to think on." He smashed his fist on the boat's planking.

There was a sound of splintering wood. From his hiding place behind a pile of greasy rope, Toby could see Bob's shadow in the moonlight. He saw the head tip back and the outline of a bottle upturned against the yellow glow of the riverside gas lamps.

Black Bob coughed and wiped his sleeve across his mouth. Then he slumped against the tiller and almost asleep, he steered the

boat upriver on the evening tide.

Toby shivered in the bitter wind and thin icy drizzle. For two years this stinking boat had been his prison. Now he had finally worked out how he could escape. It was risky. But it was a risk he had to take.

Somewhere on the other side of the river, a clock chimed nine times. Toby pulled his ragged jacket up around his neck and waited.

It was Saturday night. Every Saturday

Black Bob went on shore and sold whatever he had been able to steal from the cargoes he had carried all week. With the money, he bought rum – fiery, black rum that came from the navy ships docked further down the Thames. Then he tied up to his mooring, chained Toby to the cross-planks and drank every last drop.

Toby closed his eyes and thought of how he had lived for the last two years. Every day, in between deliveries, Black Bob tied a rope around Toby's middle and pushed him over the side to look for scrap

metal in the stinking Thames mud. If he found something, he was fed. If he didn't, he went hungry.

Toby clenched his teeth. It was all his Uncle Michael's doing. Two years ago he had appeared at Toby's cottage. He had good news, he claimed. He knew of a cabinet maker in London who wanted an apprentice. Uncle Michael asked if Toby would accept the job.

A lump rose in Toby's throat as he remembered his mother's joy.

"It's a chance to make a new life, son," she had whispered even though there

were tears in her eyes. "You go. We'll look out for ourselves."

Toby remembered his own square-shouldered promise. "I'll send a sixpence home, ma. You wait and see." Because, as an apprentice, he'd soon be earning a bit of money.

The lump grew in Toby's throat but he didn't cry. He had stopped crying the moment after Michael had dumped him on Black Bob's cargo boat and sold him for exactly a sixpence.

Toby crept out from behind the rope and crawled over to the shore side of the

boat. Over the slap and trickle of the water against the hull, he could hear Black Bob snoring.

Across the river, ten chimes rang out. Toby felt his stomach tighten with nerves. Any minute now, Oyster Jim's barge would pass within a couple feet of them.

Oyster Jim carried a small sail which took him up river faster than Black Bob's cargo boat. But even more important, he moored a good mile away.

Every Saturday, Toby had watched Oyster Jim slide past them after the ten bells rang out. And little by little a plan had taken hold in his mind.

As the two boats passed near each other, he would jump onto Jim's barge and hide. When the barge slowed down to tie up, somehow he would scramble on shore.

Toby felt fear lurch in his guts. He knew that if he fell into the water he would drown. Worse, he knew that if Black Bob tracked him down, his life would not be worth living.

The moon slid from behind the clouds. At the tiller, Black Bob was still snoring. The tide under his feet told him all he needed to know to steer the boat.

Toby slithered silently over the edge of the boat. Then he held onto a rusty iron ring and braced his feet against the hull.

Slowly the flickering lantern that hung from the prow of Oyster Jim's barge drew closer to Black Bob's boat.

Toby waited until the two boats were

almost touching. Then, saying the only
prayer he knew – *God Help Me* – he
jumped across the oily water.

Thump! Toby landed heavily beside a pile of dirty rags. As fast as he could he scrambled underneath them and curled up like a hedgehog.

Even though Oyster Jim hated Black

Bob, Toby knew he would hand him back if there was a penny to be made.

"Wozzat?" growled a drunken voice.

A greasy head appeared through a hatch.

Toby held his breath. The head was

just in front of him. A sharp beaky face looked around.

"Nuffink," muttered Oyster Jim. "Pour us another noggin, you daft lump."

The head disappeared and the hatch slammed shut.

In the darkness Toby let out his breath. For the first time he was grateful that almost every man on the river drank themselves stupid most nights.

Half an hour later, Toby crawled from

under the pile of rags over the side of
Oyster Jim's barge, and got ready to jump
again. In front of him a line of rickety
wooden poles grew out of the oily black
water. Rough planks nailed across them
formed a kind of ladder up onto the bank.

Toby muttered his prayer, grabbed
hold of a wooden plank and hung on for
dear life.

"You didn't ought to be there," said a
raspy voice above him.

Toby's stomach went cold.

Tears welled up in his eyes. It was all over.

"Heh," said the voice. "Gimme your hand. It's dangerous round 'ere. I'll help you."

2

A New Friend

"Well I never!" The raspy voice had
turned into a boy the same age as Toby.
He had a bright cunning look to his face
and a wide friendly grin. "You look like
a mud puppy!"

Toby was so relieved that he hadn't

been grabbed by the throat and dragged
back down the river, he couldn't speak.

"Jack Riley's my name," said the boy.
"There ain't nothing I don't know around
here." He grinned again. "'Cept you
of course."

Toby straightened up and introduced
himself to Jack.

"Mmm," said Jack when Toby had

finished the story of his life in two minutes.

"When was the last time you ate, then?"

"Two days ago," said Toby. As he spoke he suddenly felt horribly weak and hungry.

"That's disgustin', that is," said Jack. He put his hand on Toby's shoulder.

"You follow me, young Toby." He laughed and held his fingers to his nose.

"But not too close, mind. Not till we get you a new suit of clothes."

Toby stared at him.

"But how can we do that? It's late and I haven't a farthing."

Jack laughed. "Time don't matter and no-one has any money." He held up a stubby finger as if
he was testing the wind. "Good drying weather, though, now the rain has
stopped. Come on."

Toby followed Jack down a narrow cobbled alley, across a muddy street and into a crumbling stone courtyard.

By now a good breeze was blowing and sure enough damp clothes were hanging out of the windows to dry.

Toby watched in amazement as Jack
shinnied up the side of the houses and

one by one snatched a pair of trousers, a
shirt, and a jacket. He was just about to
grab a thick blanket when a woman's face
appeared at the window.

"Thief!" she bawled at the top of her

voice. "Stop, thief!" There was a sound of doors slamming.

Jack landed like a cat and zig-zagged back down the alley.

Toby ran after him, trying as hard as he could to stop his muddy feet from slipping on the cobblestones.

Ten minutes later, Jack and Toby ducked through a broken wooden gate and threw themselves on the ground. As they

waited in the darkness, Toby pulled off
his rags and began to rub at the mud
that covered his arms and legs. It was a
hopeless job.

"Hold on," said Jack. He pointed
across the yard. "I think I see just what
you need."

In a corner half hidden by shadow was
a large wooden rain barrel. Jack got up
and put his hand inside it.

"How about a wash
before dinner?"

Toby peered through the tavern window. Inside it was crowded and noisy and full of smoke. But at least it was warm.

"How will we get food in here?" he asked

Beside him, Jack cocked his head. "Fancy your chances begging?"

The thought of squeezing through a roomful of drunks, begging for money made Toby feel sick. But he was so hungry, he felt sick anyway.

"Thing about drunks," said Jack as they pushed through the doorway and found a place in the corner, "is they're either mean or soppy."

"What do you mean, soppy?" said Toby. All the drunks he had ever known were either mean, very mean or violent and mean.

"Slobbering on about how things were better when they was younger," muttered Jack. "You know. All soft in the head."

He pointed. "Look at that one."

Toby looked. A red-nosed man in a worn jacket sat on a bench with his back to the wall. In front of him was an almost empty bottle.

Every few minutes a huge sigh passed through the man's large body and he slumped lower against the wall. Finally he bowed his head and wiped his nose with his sleeve.

"What did I tell you!" said Jack triumphantly. "Soppy as they come."

He gave Toby a shove. "Go on. Get a farthing out of him before he drinks it."

Toby bit his lip. "What should I say," he whispered.

Jack rolled his eyes. "How about 'Got a farthing for a hungry lad, guv'nor?'"

Toby got up and dodged around swaying bodies.

"Excuse me, guv'nor," he whispered to the red-faced man. "Can you spare a farthing for a hungry boy?"

The man looked up. He reached into his pocket and pulled the linings inside out. Nothing.

"'Ave a drink, instead," he muttered and held up the almost empty bottle.

At that moment there was a crash of broken glass and everyone went quiet.

In the middle of the

room a short, tubby man with round gold glasses and a moustache was standing in front of a huge black-bearded sailor.

The tubby man was waving a black book.

The sailor was waving a broken chair.

"My name is Thomas Barnardo," cried the little man. "I have come to spread the word of the Lord." He held up the book in his hand. "Listen to the Lord's message. His kindness is your salvation."

"Chuck 'im out!" cackled a woman in a torn scarlet dress.

"We don't want none of your palaver 'ere," yelled a grimy weaselly-looking man. "Toss your book on the fire."

A loud guffaw went round the room.

To Toby's astonishment the little man climbed onto a table and shouted louder. "Be kind to your neighbour and the Lord will be kind to you."

"So what?" bellowed the huge sailor and with one meaty hand, he picked up the little man and lifted him off the floor.

Another chair went over and more bottles smashed.

Suddenly Toby found himself staring into the eyes of the

little man with the gold glasses. They were blazing. But not with anger, Toby realized with a jolt. It was something else.

A hand grabbed his collar. "Let's get out of 'ere," shouted Jack. "The constables are coming!"

Toby and Jack lowered their heads and shoved through the broken tables and wrestling bodies. A minute later, they were in the street.

The sound of whistles grew louder.

"You there! Stop!"

For the second time that night, Jack and Toby ran for their lives.

3

A Light in the Darkness

It was Toby who saw her first.

He and Jack were hiding in a stable
yard when they heard the creak of wooden
wheels. Toby put his head over the wall.
An old woman was pushing a cart piled
with baked potatoes.

"Let's ask if she's got any broken ones," whispered Toby.

"Don't be daft," said Jack. "You  pretend you're sick and while she's not looking, I'll grab two big ones."

Toby swallowed. "What if someone sees ...?"

"They won't," said Jack.

With a pounding heart, Toby clutched his stomach and stumbled down the street.

"Ma'am! Ma'am!"

The old lady stopped her cart. In the murky street light, her round face was as

wrinkled as an oak apple. She smiled at
the two boys.

"You young 'uns look starved!" she
said kindly. "Take these!"

Then to Jack and Toby's amazement,
she handed them each a big potato and
set off down the cobbled street.

Neither Toby and Jack moved. It was

almost as if they had forgotten that
kindness existed anywhere.

"Let's go back to the stables,"

whispered Toby. Somehow the potato was too precious to eat in the street.

A wide grin spread across Jack's face. "Just what I was thinking, mate."

The stables were warm and steamy from the two horses tethered inside.

Toby and Jack kicked some straw into a corner and made themselves a bed. Then they ate half a potato each and fell into a deep sleep.

★ ★ ★

Toby awoke with a jerk.

A lantern was swinging above his head.
In the bright circle of light, Toby saw the
dark shapes of two men. He felt in the
straw beside him. Jack was gone.

Toby's mind exploded with terror.
"Don't kill me," he screamed. He felt
for the potato in his pockets. "Take this.
It's all I have."
One of the men bent down and laid his

hand on Toby's shoulder.

"We don't want your food, lad," he said. "We are here in the Lord's name. We want to help you."

Toby stared into the man's face. He had a moustache and wore round gold glasses. For a split second he wondered if he was dreaming. "You're the man I saw in the tavern," he gasped.

The little man looked grave and turned to his companion.

"It is a terrible thing that a lad so young should be in such an evil place, Mr. Williams," he said. "Now do you see why my work is so important?"

"Indeed, I do,"

replied the man holding the lantern.
"Come lad, we will give you food and a
roof over your head."

Toby didn't move. He stared into the
tubby man's face.

"How do I know
you aren't lying?
How do I know you
won't sell me back
to Black Bob?"

The little man held
Toby's thin dirty hand.

"My name is
Thomas Barnardo.
I have a house for
homeless children."
He spoke gently.
"I come in kindness.
Let me help you."

Kindness. Toby's bottom lip began to

tremble. Suddenly, the terrible despair of the last two years welled up like a fountain inside him.

He crumpled into a heap and sobbed his heart out.

Up in the rafters Jack Riley clenched his teeth and didn't move. There was no way a grown-up was taking him off. Jack

didn't trust grown ups. He'd heard too
many of their lies.

Below the two men helped Toby to
his feet.

"I need Jack," cried Toby in a choked
voice. "He's my friend."

Up in the darkness, a prickling feeling
crawled over Jack's body. No-one had
ever said they needed him. Jack bit his lip.
Maybe they would never say it again.

As George Williams pulled open the
stable door, Jack knew he didn't want to
be on his own anymore. He needed Toby
as much as Toby needed him.

He let go of
the rafter and
dropped
onto the straw.

"Well done,
lad," said

Thomas Barnardo as if he was used to
boys dropping out of nowhere. He put his
hand on Jack's shoulder.

"Hot cocoa all round tonight, don't
you think, Mr. Williams?"

George Williams pulled the stable door
shut behind them.

"Capital idea, Dr. Barnardo,"
he replied.

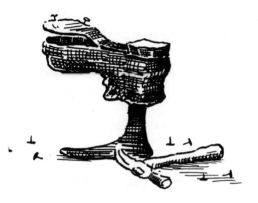

4

Two Helping Hands

Thomas Barnardo stood in front of the house that was his home for children and said a small prayer to himself. Through the window, he could see Jack Riley and Toby Cutler hammering soles onto a big pile of old boots.

"Those two lads are doing well," he murmured to George Williams, standing beside him.

"They're good boys," agreed George Williams. "The others like 'em, too."

Thomas Barnardo looked over his glasses. "I've noticed that too," he said slowly. "It's given me an idea."

The two men walked through the house and round to the back yard.

Everywhere children were sorting clothes,
cleaning pots and chopping wood.

"We have over a hundred children
here at Hope Place," muttered Thomas
Barnardo as if he was talking to himself.

"Some are old enough to work
for other people and make money for
the home."

"But who could organise them?" asked
George Williams. "We haven't a free

moment between us."

Thomas Barnardo smiled.

"I know two boys who could help."

"You mean Toby Cutler and Jack Riley?"

"Exactly," replied Thomas Barnardo.

★ ★ ★

Five minutes later Toby Cutler and Jack Riley stood in front of Thomas Barnardo's desk.

"Nothing's wrong is there, sir," muttered Jack. Both he and Toby were so frightened, their knees were knocking. They had been at Hope Place for just over a month now and their lives had changed completely.

For the first time ever, they had breakfast in the morning and supper at night. They had a bed to sleep on and once a week there was reading and

writing. On Sundays, Dr. Barnardo even read to them from the Bible.

Of course, there was hard work too, but Toby and Jack were good at hard work.

Toby bit his lip. "You ain't gonna throw us out, are you, sir?"

"Throw you out? I never throw anyone out," replied Thomas Barnardo with a smile. "Especially not two of the cleverest boys in Hope Place."

He leaned back on his chair and looked very serious. "I need your help. We have to find a way of making money for the home."

Toby felt as if he was ten feet tall. He would never forget that he owed all his new-found happiness to this kind and extraordinary man.

"I want to start a business selling chopped wood, Toby," said Thomas Barnardo. "And I believe you could be be useful to me."

Toby went bright pink.

"I'll do anything I can, sir," he almost whispered.

"Excellent."

Thomas Barnardo pressed his fingers together and turned to Jack.

"You know London like the back of your hand, don't you Jack?"

"Yes sir."

"Will you help me start a message delivery service?"

Jack's face lit up. "I know all the short cuts," he almost shouted. "I'll show you."

"Not me," replied Thomas Barnardo, smiling. "Choose your boys."

"They've got to be good runners," said Jack gruffly. "I'll test 'em myself."

Thomas Barnardo looked at the two boys who only a month before had been as wild and skinny as a pair of alley cats.

With God's will, he would help hundreds more children just like them.

5

God Bless Dr. Barnardo's Boys!

Toby Cutler wanted to pinch himself. Was he really driving a proper pony trap with Jack sitting beside him? Or was it a dream?

Toby Cutler did pinch himself. It wasn't a dream! He then pinched Jack just for the fun of it.

"Ow!" cried Jack. "What did you do that for, Toby!"

"It's not a dream!" shouted Toby. He threw back his head and laughed. "We're really here!"

Jack pretended to look bad-tempered.

"We won't be anywhere if you don't follow my instructions," he muttered gruffly. "Turn left by that pillar box."

But inside Jack was just as excited as Toby. It was two years almost to the day

since Thomas Barnardo had asked them
to help raise money for the home. And
over those two years, the chopped wood
business and messenger service had been
a huge success.

Thomas Barnardo had bought another
home and was even trying to raise money
so that he could buy a tavern and turn it
into a meeting place.

This afternoon, as a mark of their
standing in the home, Toby and Jack had

been allowed to make a special delivery of chopped wood to a cabinet maker on the other side of London.

Jack punched his friend lightly on the arm. "Who would have thought it, eh?" he said. "Two starved runts like us driving about like toffs in our own wagon."

Toby grinned and tried to concentrate on guiding the pony down the crowded noisy street.

"There it is!" cried Jack pointing to the end of the street. Beyond a market stall, a flaky sign hung halfway up a brick house. SAM DAWKINS CABINET MAKER.

They turned the wagon under the sign and went into a yard.

A woman in a checked apron hurried out of the brick house. She had rosy cheeks and her brown hair was twisted into a bun. "Dr. Barnardo's boys?" she asked.

Toby and Jack nodded and jumped down from the cart.

"Which of you is Toby Cutler?"

"Me, ma'am," replied Toby quickly. "Is something wrong."

"Not at all, lad," replied the woman "Mr. Dawkins would like a word when you're finished."

"Must be another order," muttered Toby as he began to unstack the wood.

A sixth sense told Jack that it wasn't. It was something else.

Toby had a way with wood. Only last week Dr. Barnardo himself had mentioned it.

"Do you ever think about being an apprentice?" asked Jack in an easy voice. "You know, like you thought you was going to be once."

Toby's eyes lit up. "All the time," he replied. "Then I could send my ma a sixpence like I promised. He shrugged. "But anyone can dream."

At that moment, a thick set man with

grizzled grey hair walked briskly into the yard. He wore a long leather apron with tools tucked into the leather pockets.

"Sam Dawkins," he said in a deep voice. He held out his hand to both boys.

Then he looked Toby firmly in the eye.

"I need an apprentice, Toby," said Sam Dawkins. "Dr. Barnardo says you're the lad for the job." He looked Toby straight in the eye. "Will you work for me?"

Toby was too stunned to speak.

"Yes," muttered Jack kicking him in the shins.

"Yes," cried Toby. "Yes, please!"

Sam Dawkins smiled.

"You start tomorrow."

★ ★ ★

Thomas Barnardo leaned back on his office chair. Beside him, his assistant George Williams watched as a young girl poured out four cups of tea.

"We shall celebrate with tea, Mr. Williams," said Dr. Barnardo with a smile. He motioned with his hand for Jack Riley and Toby Cutler to sit down.

Jack picked up his tea cup and almost spilt it. He was still trying hard to feel happy for Toby. But it wasn't working. The truth was he would miss his friend dreadfully.

"Cheer up, Jack," said Dr. Barnardo. "I've got a surprise for you, too." He picked up a letter. "The post office want you to work for them. You can lodge at Sam Dawkins'."

Jack's world turned upside down. So did his cup of tea. He watched

in slow motion as Dr. Barnardo passed him a letter across his desk.

"Well?"

Jack was too stunned to speak.

"Yes," muttered Toby kicking Jack in the shins.

"Yes," shouted Jack. "Yes! Yes! Thank you sir!"

"Don't thank me," replied Dr. Barnardo. "You have both been a great credit to me. Your hard work has brought its own rewards."

Thomas Barnardo lifted his cup.

"Mr. Williams," he cried. "These fine fellows are the starving urchins we found in a stable! Do you recognize them, sir?"

Jack and Toby looked at each other and grinned. They did indeed look completely different but they knew they would never forget that first night on the river.

Toby swallowed and spoke in the deepest voice he could manage.

"It is all your doing, sir," he said. "God bless you, sir."

"Well said," cried George Williams. He raised his cup first to Dr. Barnardo and then to Jack and Toby.

"God bless Dr. Barnardo's Boys!"

Notes

Dr. Barnardo

Thomas Barnardo set up the first refuge for homeless boys in 1867. It was called the East End Juvenille Mission. The boys worked at chopping wood, brushmaking, bootmaking and delivering messages to raise money for their keep. Dr. Barnardo went on to open many more homes and helped thousands of orphaned and homeless children.

London's East End

Only poor people lived in the East End of London in Victorian times. It was an overcrowded slum area. Diseases like cholera and typhoid spread easily because there was no clean water and no sewage system. More than half the children died before they were five years old.

Hard Times

In the 1850s 'stink' industries like glue and rubber factories moved into the East End. Conditions were terrible and dangerous and many men were killed. Women often did 'piece work' at home, sewing parts of garments.

Street Life

Street lighting came from gas lamps. A lamplighter went around each evening lighting the street lamps and turning them off in the morning. The East End was badly lit and bands of thieves roamed the streets picking pockets and stealing what they could to eat.

Foodsellers

Many people tried to make a living by selling food on the street. Hot potatoes cost less than a penny and were popular since poor people did not have an oven at home.

Sparks: Historical Adventures

ANCIENT GREECE
The Great Horse of Troy – The Trojan War
0 7496 3369 7 (hbk)   0 7496 3538 X (pbk)
The Winner's Wreath – Ancient Greek Olympics
0 7496 3368 9 (hbk)   0 7496 3555 X (pbk)

INVADERS AND SETTLERS
Boudicca Strikes Back – The Romans in Britain
0 7496 3366 2 (hbk)   0 7496 3546 0 (pbk)
Viking Raiders – A Norse Attack
0 7496 3089 2 (hbk)   0 7496 3457 X (pbk)
Erik's New Home – A Viking Town
0 7496 3367 0 (hbk)   0 7496 3552 5 (pbk)
TALES OF THE ROWDY ROMANS
The Great Necklace Hunt
0 7496 2221 0 (hbk)   0 7496 2628 3 (pbk)
The Lost Legionary
0 7496 2222 9 (hbk)   0 7496 2629 1 (pbk)
The Guard Dog Geese
0 7496 2331 4 (hbk)   0 7496 2630 5 (pbk)
A Runaway Donkey
0 7496 2332 2 (hbk)   0 7496 2631 3 (pbk)

TUDORS AND STUARTS
Captain Drake's Orders – The Armada
0 7496 2556 2 (hbk)   0 7496 3121 X (pbk)
London's Burning – The Great Fire of London
0 7496 2557 0 (hbk)   0 7496 3122 8 (pbk)
Mystery at the Globe – Shakespeare's Theatre
0 7496 3096 5 (hbk)   0 7496 3449 9 (pbk)
Plague! – A Tudor Epidemic
0 7496 3365 4 (hbk)   0 7496 3556 8 (pbk)
Stranger in the Glen – Rob Roy
0 7496 2586 4 (hbk)   0 7496 3123 6 (pbk)
A Dream of Danger – The Massacre of Glencoe
0 7496 2587 2 (hbk)   0 7496 3124 4 (pbk)
A Queen's Promise – Mary Queen of Scots
0 7496 2589 9 (hbk)   0 7496 3125 2 (pbk)
Over the Sea to Skye – Bonnie Prince Charlie
0 7496 2588 0 (hbk)   0 7496 3126 0 (pbk)
TALES OF A TUDOR TEARAWAY
A Pig Called Henry
0 7496 2204 4 (hbk)   0 7496 2625 9 (pbk)
A Horse Called Deathblow
0 7496 2205 9 (hbk)   0 7496 2624 0 (pbk)
Dancing for Captain Drake
0 7496 2234 2 (hbk)   0 7496 2626 7 (pbk)
Birthdays are a Serious Business
0 7496 2235 0 (hbk)   0 7496 2627 5 (pbk)

VICTORIAN ERA
The Runaway Slave – The British Slave Trade
0 7496 3093 0 (hbk)   0 7496 3456 1 (pbk)
The Sewer Sleuth – Victorian Cholera
0 7496 2590 2 (hbk)   0 7496 3128 7 (pbk)
Convict! – Criminals Sent to Australia
0 7496 2591 0 (hbk)   0 7496 3129 5 (pbk)
An Indian Adventure – Victorian India
0 7496 3090 6 (hbk)   0 7496 3451 0 (pbk)
Farewell to Ireland – Emigration to America
0 7496 3094 9 (hbk)   0 7496 3448 0 (pbk)

The Great Hunger – Famine in Ireland
0 7496 3095 7 (hbk)   0 7496 3447 2 (pbk)
Fire Down the Pit – A Welsh Mining Disaster
0 7496 3091 4 (hbk)   0 7496 3450 2 (pbk)
Tunnel Rescue – The Great Western Railway
0 7496 3353 0 (hbk)   0 7496 3537 1 (pbk)
Kidnap on the Canal – Victorian Waterways
0 7496 3352 2 (hbk)   0 7496 3540 1 (pbk)
Dr. Barnardo's Boys – Victorian Charity
0 7496 3358 1 (hbk)   0 7496 3541 X (pbk)
The Iron Ship – Brunel's Great Britain
0 7496 3355 7 (hbk)   0 7496 3543 6 (pbk)
Bodies for Sale – Victorian Tomb-Robbers
0 7496 3364 6 (hbk)   0 7496 3539 8 (pbk)
Penny Post Boy – The Victorian Postal Service
0 7496 3362 X (hbk)   0 7496 3544 4 (pbk)
The Canal Diggers – The Manchester Ship Canal
0 7496 3356 5 (hbk)   0 7496 3545 2 (pbk)
The Tay Bridge Tragedy – A Victorian Disaster
0 7496 3354 9 (hbk)   0 7496 3547 9 (pbk)
Stop, Thief! – The Victorian Police
0 7496 3359 X (hbk)   0 7496 3548 7 (pbk)
A School – for Girls! – Victorian Schools
0 7496 3360 3 (hbk)   0 7496 3549 5 (pbk)
Chimney Charlie – Victorian Chimney Sweeps
0 7496 3351 4 (hbk)   0 7496 3551 7 (pbk)
Down the Drain – Victorian Sewers
0 7496 3357 3 (hbk)   0 7496 3550 9 (pbk)
The Ideal Home – A Victorian New Town
0 7496 3361 1 (hbk)   0 7496 3553 3 (pbk)
Stage Struck – Victorian Music Hall
0 7496 3363 8 (hbk)   0 7496 3554 1 (pbk)
TRAVELS OF A YOUNG VICTORIAN
The Golden Key
0 7496 2360 8 (hbk)   0 7496 2632 1 (pbk)
Poppy's Big Push
0 7496 2361 6 (hbk)   0 7496 2633 X (pbk)
Poppy's Secret
0 7496 2374 8 (hbk)   0 7496 2634 8 (pbk)
The Lost Treasure
0 7496 2375 6 (hbk)   0 7496 2635 6 (pbk)

20th-CENTURY HISTORY
Fight for the Vote – The Suffragettes
0 7496 3092 2 (hbk)   0 7496 3452 9 (pbk)
The Road to London – The Jarrow March
0 7496 2609 7 (hbk)   0 7496 3132 5 (pbk)
The Sandbag Secret – The Blitz
0 7496 2608 9 (hbk)   0 7496 3133 3 (pbk)
Sid's War – Evacuation
0 7496 3209 7 (hbk)   0 7496 3445 6 (pbk)
D-Day! – Wartime Adventure
0 7496 3208 9 (hbk)   0 7496 3446 4 (pbk)
The Prisoner – A Prisoner of War
0 7496 3212 7 (hbk)   0 7496 3455 3 (pbk)
Escape from Germany – Wartime Refugees
0 7496 3211 9 (hbk)   0 7496 3454 5 (pbk)
Flying Bombs – Wartime Bomb Disposal
0 7496 3210 0 (hbk)   0 7496 3453 7 (pbk)
12,000 Miles From Home – Sent to Australia
0 7496 3370 0 (hbk)   0 7496 3542 8 (pbk)